You're The Biggest

When the baby arrived, your very important job began.

You became
THE BIGGEST.
Only you are special
enough to be the biggest.

You will have to teach
the baby so many things,
like . . .

how to share . . .

how to explore . . .

how to be

brave ...

how to ask

questions . . .

and how to

search for answers.

How to
be a good
friend ...

how to make

the best of things . . .

how to reach for the stars . . .

and how to run and jump.

You will always have someone to share your secrets...

and share

your dreams.

You are going
to have so much fun
together.

The baby
is very lucky
to have you as

THE BIGGEST!

You will always be a hero.
You will always have
a friend.

You're The Biggest first published by Forget Me Not Books, an imprint of **FROM YOU TO ME LTD**, February 2017.
FROM YOU TO ME, Waterhouse, Waterhouse Lane, Monkton Combe, Bath, BA2 7JA, UK

For a full range of all our titles where journals & books can also be personalised, please visit

WWW.FROMYOUTOME.COM

Written and illustrated by Lucy Tapper & Steve Wilson fromlucy.com

9 11 13 15 14 12 10 8

Printed and bound in China. This paper is manufactured from pulp
sourced from forests that are legally and sustainably managed.

Also available:
Welcome to the World